MONSTER BUDDIES

I'M A FIRE BREATHER!

MEET A DRAGON

Shannon Knudsen

illustrated by Renée Kurilla

MILLBROOK PRESS • MINNEAPOLIS

For Scott, conqueror of the Dragon's Lair —SK

For all the new (dragon) babies in my life:
Sydney, Micah, and Landon —RK

Millbrook Press
A division of Lerner Publishing Group, Inc.
241 First Avenue North
Minneapolis, MN 55401 USA

For reading levels and more information, look up this title at www.lernerbooks.com.

Main body text set in Sunshine Regular 17/24.
Typeface provided by Chank.

Library of Congress Cataloging-in-Publication Data

Knudsen, Shannon, 1971–
    I'm a fire breather: meet a dragon / by Shannon Knudsen.
      pages   cm. — (Monster buddies)
    ISBN 978-0-7613-9190-6 (lib. bdg. : alk. paper)
    ISBN 978-1-4677-4777-6 (eBook)
    1. Dragons. I. Title.
  GR830.D7Z35 2015
  398.24'54—dc23   2013027528

Manufactured in the United States of America
1 – BOL – 7/15/14

TABLE of CONTENTS

Meet a Dragon

I soar through the sky like a giant lizard with wings. The sun reflects off my hard, shiny skin. I breathe a stream of fire.

My name is Alice. I am a dragon, and you are quite lucky to meet me.

If you don't know what a dragon is, I feel sorry for you. But don't worry.

I'll tell you all about us.

Fame and Fortune

Dragons are famous. Why?
It's simple.

We're huge.

We're smart.

We have piles of treasure.

We breathe fire.
And we're very,
very hard to kill.

Of course, we aren't real. You humans tell
stories about us. But you'll never meet
one of us in real life. Sad, isn't it?

Where do dragons come from? We hatch from eggs. Meet my children: William, Cecily, and Ralph. Lovely, aren't they? Each of them will live for hundreds of years.

Like all dragons, my children are quite clever. Once they tricked a little girl into thinking they wanted to be friends. She followed them all the way home. Then they ate her. **Adorable!**

My babies and I have our own castle. Come inside! As you can see, I like to live in style. The place once belonged to a knight. He was quite tasty.

That's right. Dragons eat people. I prefer mine toasted, with plenty of mustard.

That doesn't mean we go looking for humans, though. In fact, many dragons live in caves far away from people. Why do you suppose that is?

Lonely caves and castles are perfect hiding places for treasure. Dragons love shiny things. If it glitters, a dragon wants it. I'm quite fond of rubies. But my hoard has plenty of gold, silver, and every kind of gem.

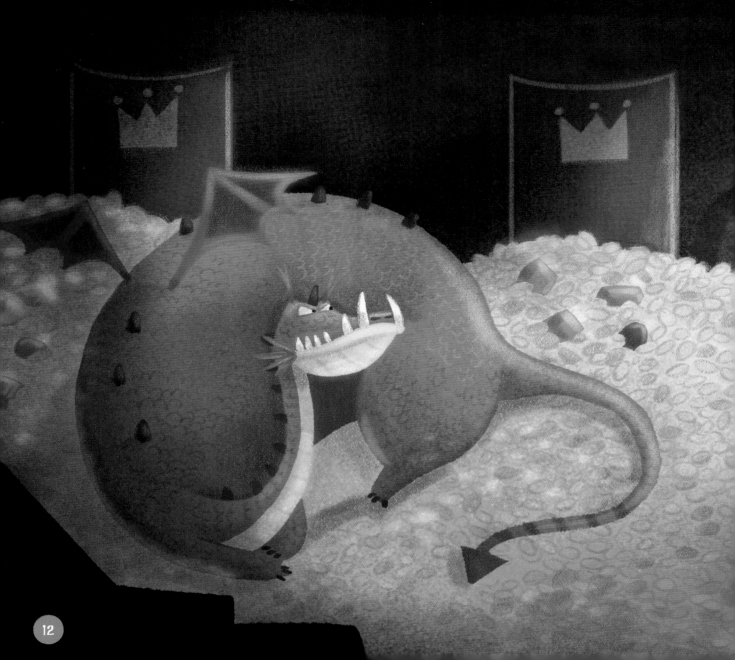

Guarding my treasure is a full-time job. Nothing is worse than gathering rubies from all over the world, only to have some pesky human steal them!

Humans make other problems for dragons too.
Sometimes heroes even go on quests to try to kill us.
And you call us troublemakers!

It's a good thing dragons have such hard scales. You would need a very sharp sword to pierce my skin. And if you tried, I would just fly away or use my fire breath. Time for brunch!

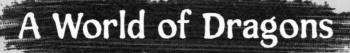

A World of Dragons

Dragons like me usually live in Europe. Some European dragons have just two legs, but they get around fine. A few have extra heads. They can put on quite a fireworks show!

I also have cousins all over the world. This is Cheng, a dragon from China. Chinese dragons have no wings, but they fly quite well without them. They don't breathe fire, either. Instead, they control water! Chinese dragons can move rivers, lakes, and even the ocean. These dragons can bring rain to dry land. Or they can bring a flood.

In China, people believe dragons bring good luck. During Chinese New Year, people carry a huge dragon costume on poles and do a dance named after us. That's much better than trying to kill us, if you ask me!

People in Vietnam are fans of dragons too. An old Vietnamese story tells of a dragon king who fell in love with a fairy. Their children were the first humans!

Dragons Rule

As you can see, we dragons truly are the kings and queens of the monster world. Wouldn't you like to thank me for sharing our secrets?

Of course you would!

First, pass the mustard. Thank you.
Now, stand still while I take
a nice, big breath...

A Dragon's Day Writing Activity

You've learned a lot about dragons. It's time to show off your treasure trove of dragon smarts. Grab a pencil and a piece of paper. Write a short story about what a dragon's day is like. What does the dragon do for fun? Does it fly to visit other dragons? Does it toast marshmallows with its fire breath? Draw a picture to go with your story.

GLOSSARY

dragon: a flying monster that looks like a large lizard. Some dragons have wings and breathe fire.

hatch: to break out of an egg

hoard: a bunch of gold, silver, and gems that a dragon keeps in a safe place

quests: long trips people take to perform important tasks

scales: hard, shiny plates that cover a dragon's skin

treasure: gold, silver, and gems that are worth lots of money

TO LEARN MORE

Books

Bar-el, Dan. *Not Your Typical Dragon.* New York: Viking Juvenile, 2013. When Crispin turns seven and tries to breathe fire, he gets whipped cream instead! Find out how a young dragon deals with being different in this funny picture book.

Caldwell, Stella. *Dragonworld: Secrets of the Dragon Domain.* Philadelphia: Running Kids Press, 2011. Learn more about different types of dragons, where they would live, and what they would do if they were real.

Eversole, Robyn. *East Dragon, West Dragon.* New York: Atheneum Books for Young Readers, 2012. East Dragon and West Dragon are not the same. That's why they're scared of each other. But do they have to be? Read this picture book to find out.

Nesbit, E. *The Book of Dragons.* New York: Random House, 2010. In this book of short stories, dragons shape the fates of princes, queens, and ordinary children.

Websites

China Family Adventure: Dragons
http://www.china-family-adventure.com/chinese-dragons.html
Learn more about Chinese dragons. Then explore the rest of this website to find out about Chinese holidays, traditions, and more.

Komodo Dragons
http://kids.nationalgeographic.com/kids/animals/creaturefeature/komodo-dragon
Komodo dragons don't fly or breathe fire, but they are the biggest lizards on Earth. Check out photos and fast facts here. Watch a video of baby Komodo dragons hatching and growing up!

INDEX